LVL: 3⟩

Break a Sea Leg, Shrimp-Breath!

Barnacle Barb & Her Pirate Crew

Written by Nadia Higgins
Illustrated by Jimmy Holder

magic wagon

For Yvette, my crazy giggler

visit us at www.abdopublishing.com

Published by Magic Wagon, a division of the ABDO Publishing Group, 8000 West 78th Street, Edina, Minnesota 55439.
Copyright © 2008 by Abdo Consulting Group, Inc. International copyrights reserved in all countries. All rights reserved.
No part of this book may be reproduced in any form without written permission from the publisher.
Looking Glass Library™ is a trademark and logo of Magic Wagon.

Printed in the United States.

Text by Nadia Higgins
Illustrations by Jimmy Holder
Edited by Bob Temple
Interior layout and design by Emily Love
Cover design by Emily Love

Library of Congress Cataloging-in-Publication Data
Higgins, Nadia.
  Break a sea leg, shrimp-breath! / Nadia Higgins ; illustrated by Jimmy Holder.
    p. cm. — (Barnacle Barb & her pirate crew)
  ISBN 978-1-60270-092-5
  [1. Pirates—Fiction. 2. Talent shows—Fiction.] I. Holder, Jimmy, ill. II. Title.
PZ7.H5349558Br 2008
[E]—dc22
                        2007036978

"Ack! Eeeeeeeee! Ooooooooow!" Stinkin' Jim howled like a dogfish.

"What's the trouble, Stinkin'?" Shrimp-Breath Sherman said, looking up from his magazine.

"Oh, 'tis just Ol' Planky," Stinkin' said. Shrimp-Breath noticed that Stinkin' was doing the most dreaded chore aboard their pirate ship—swabbing the plank.

"'Tis a frightful plank indeed," Shrimp-Breath Sherman said. "What with all the splintery cracks and knuckle-grabbin' snares."

"True, true, me hearty," Stinkin' Jim said. He yanked a bloody splinter out of his palm. "I'd give me lucky parrot feather for a nice new plank!"

Shrimp-Breath sighed. "If only . . . ," he muttered to himself. He turned back to the page he'd been reading in his magazine.

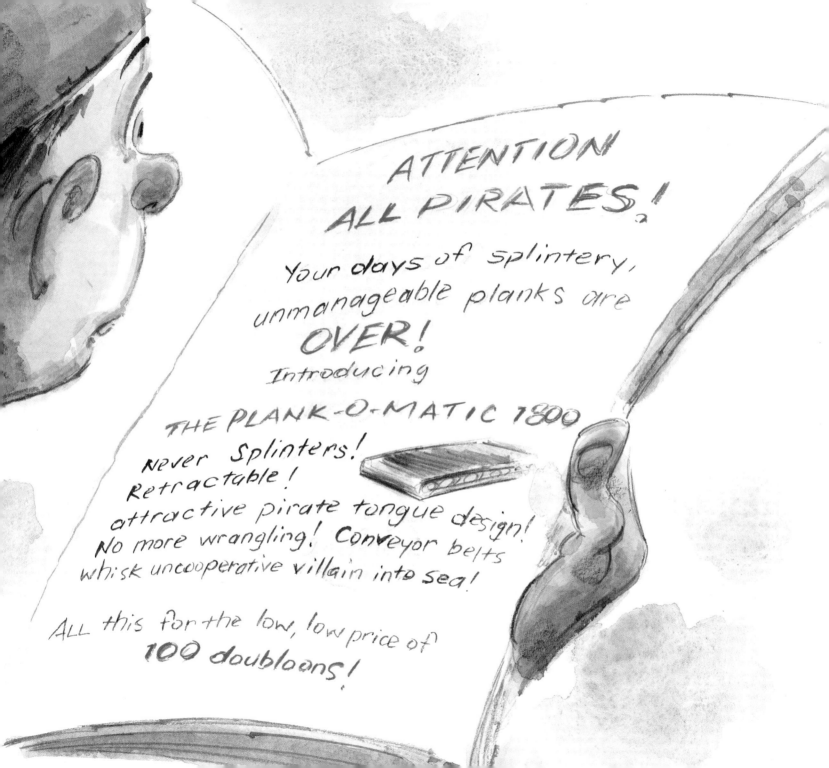

Shrimp-Breath Sherman imagined himself bringing Stinkin' Jim the Plank-o-matic 1800 with a giant red bow tied around it.

Shrimp-Breath tried reading his magazine, but he couldn't concentrate. He flipped through the pages. *One hundred doubloons. One hundred doubloons.* The words rang over and over in his head. *One hundred doubloons.*

Can you fiddle?
Tell a riddle?
Can you pick your fleas
on a flying trapeze?
Are YOU the next
SUPER STAR
OF THE SEVEN SEAS
Calling all pirates for the
talent show of the year!
First Prize: 100 doubloons

"One hundred doubloons?!" Shrimp-Breath Sherman cried. He looked again at the tattered page. Could it be? Yes, yes. There were the words, plain as muck.

"Aha!" Shrimp-Breath Sherman bounced to his feet. He had a plan!

Shrimp-Breath remembered the blue ribbon he'd won at the Pirate Fair last summer. He'd taken first prize in the balloon animals contest for his amazing balloon shrimp.

Surely he could make lots of balloon animals. He would make the masterpieces on stage. He would win the contest, take the prize money, and buy the Plank-o-matic!

Shrimp-Breath imagined his grateful friends cheering for him. In this daydream, he wore the bow like a sash. In sparkly letters, it read, "Super Star of the Seven Seas."

"Barnacle Barrrb! Armpit Arnie! Pegleg Pedro! Slimebeard!" Shrimp-Breath Sherman called the rest of the crew to the deck and told them his plan.

"'Tis genius!" Barb declared.

"Foolproof!" Pegleg seconded.

As the contest was just one week away, Shrimp-Breath would need to practice hard. He needed a place where no one would bother him.

"Clear out the closet!" Barnacle Barb ordered.

"There," Barnacle Barb said, throwing some stained socks overboard. "Here be a nice, quiet place for you, Shrimp-Breath."

She glared at the crew. "Any of you ruckus-rousers makes any hubbub for Shrimp-Breath—you'll be swabbin' Ol' Planky till she sparkles."

The pirates slinked away as quietly as sea snakes. Grabbing a stash of balloons from his pocket, Shrimp-Breath Sherman walked into the closet and shut the door.

The next week was the quietest week the crew had ever heard.

Pfffft. Squeak. Squeak. The sounds of Shrimp-Breath blowing up and twisting his balloons could be heard clear across the deck.

At last, it was the day of the contest. Shrimp-Breath Sherman peered out of the closet, blinking at the sunlight. He stood there for a long time.

"Shrimp-Breath," Pegleg Pedro said at last. "You look droopier than boiled fish whiskers."

"Never mind!" Shrimp-Breath growled. "Let's be going."

When the pirates arrived at the contest, the acts had already started. Shrimp-Breath Sherman got a sticker with his number—206. He put it on, and the pirates waited for his turn.

On stage, another contestant juggled 600 skulls. Then, a lobster trainer made his lobster stand on one claw. Another pirate did a perfect impersonation of a blowfish.

"205!" the announcer called. The act before Shrimp-Breath's was a comedy routine.

"What be Captain Hook's favorite shop?" the comedian said, his good eye winking at the audience. "The secondhand store!"

All the pirates snorted and hollered and whooped—except Shrimp-Breath Sherman. He looked around.

"I can't do it!" he yelled to Barnacle Barb. "Barrrb, Barrrb, I can't do it!"

"Frogwash!" Barnacle Barb said.

"No, no," Shrimp-Breath said. He pulled Barb in closer. "The thing is, cap'n," he whispered, "me balloon animals . . . they're . . . they're . . . they're bad."

"Aye! Bad!" Barb said.

"No, no, Barrrb. Not *bad* bad. Bad—not very good."

"Oh, Shrimp-Breath," Barnacle Barb said, hanging her arm over his shoulder. "'Tis just butterfly fish in your tummy. Methinks they call it stage fright. Even the fiercest pirates get stage fright before doin' a show."

Shrimp-Breath Sherman's eyes grew as wide as sand dollars. "Even you, Barrrb?"

"Aye. Even I!" Barb replied.

"206! . . . 206!" the announcer shouted.

Shrimp-Breath clutched his balloons. "I can do it. I can do it," he said softly.

"Break a sea leg, Shrimp-Breath!" his friends called after him as he climbed onto the stage.

Shrimp-Breath Sherman looked out over the sea of faces.

"Tonight I will be makin' me . . . uh . . . amazin' balloon animals," Shrimp-Breath said. The audience cheered, and Shrimp-Breath smiled a little.

He took out a balloon. "Me first creation will be a parrot." *Pfffft. Squeak. Squeak.* Shrimp-Breath held out his parrot, but the audience just stared at it.

"What was that supposed to be again, mate?" someone called.

"That parrot looks like . . . " another pirate said, "well, it looks like a . . . a . . . a shrimp!"

Shrimp-Breath Sherman's poodle, orangutan, and gecko looked like shrimp, too.

"Go home!" someone shouted. The audience started to boo and hiss. Then, someone pelted him with clump of seaweed.

That did it. Shrimp-Breath Sherman glared at the audience. Slowly, he picked the seaweed out of his hair. "I'll show ye, ye bunch of worthless wobbegongs," he growled.

Pfffft. Squeak. Squeak. Shrimp-Breath worked so fast his hands were a blur. He climbed up a ladder. He twirled in circles. *Squeak. Plink. Boing. Fa-la-la-la!*

When he was done, a hush of amazement fell over the audience. They gazed at the huge balloon shrimp Shrimp-Breath had made.

"I say, that shrimp looks as real as me!" one judge said.

Another judge sniffed. "Why, it even smells real!" she said.

"Yes ma'am, that's why they call me Shrimp-Breath!" the pirate said, beaming.

Shrimp-Breath Sherman didn't win first prize in the talent contest. But the judges awarded him "Star Balloon Shrimper." His prize was a roll of tape.

Late that night, Shrimp-Breath sneaked up on deck. Carefully, he rolled the tape around Ol' Planky's splintery cracks and knuckle-grabbin' snares.

When he was done, Shrimp-Breath got a giant red ribbon and tied a bow around the new Ol' Planky. "That be as good as any Plank-o-matic," he said to himself.

Pirate Booty

☘ How did a pirate come to be captain of a crew? He or she was elected. If the crew was not happy with their captain, they could vote in a new leader at any time.

☘ What did real pirates do for fun? Not much. In reality, a pirate's life was mostly hard and miserable. Most men who became pirates were sailors who had no other options. They became pirates as a way to survive.

Pirate Translations

break a sea leg — good luck (said to a performer)
doubloon — pirate money (a Spanish gold coin)
frogwash — nonsense
have butterfly fish in one's tummy — be nervous
me hearty — my friend
methinks — I think
swab the deck — mop the deck